SO-AFF-885

Trilogy of Terror

by

J.B. Stamper

SCHOLASTIC INC.
New York Toronto London Auckland
Sydney New Delhi Hong Kong

Illustrations by
Dan Park
Lisa Weber
Marcelo Baez

No part of this publication may be reproduced in whole or in part, or stored in a retrieval system, or transmitted in any form or by any means, electronic, mechanical, photocopying, recording, or otherwise, without written permission of the publisher. For information regarding permission, write to Scholastic Inc., 557 Broadway, New York, NY 10012.

Text copyright © 2012 by Scholastic Inc.
"I Dare You" Illustrations copyright © 2012 by Dan Park.
"The Cat's Meow" Illustrations copyright © 2012 by Lisa Weber.
"Chomp!" Illustrations copyright © 2012 by Scholastic Inc.
All rights reserved. Published by Scholastic Inc.
Printed in the U.S.A.

ISBN-13: 978-0-545-31859-4
ISBN-10: 0-545-31859-9
(meets NASTA specifications)

SCHOLASTIC, READ 180, and associated logos are trademarks and/or registered trademarks of Scholastic Inc.
LEXILE is a registered trademark of MetaMetrics.

4 5 6 7 8 9 10   113   20 19 18 17 16 15 14 13 12 11

Contents

Chapter 1 I Dare You 4

Chapter 2 The Cat's Meow. 14

Chapter 3 Chomp!. 24

Glossary. 32

What will Javier find inside the creepy old house?

1 | I Dare You

No one went near the old house. It sat way back from the sidewalk. Its windows were broken. Its paint was peeling. Nobody had lived there for years.

Javier and his friends passed the house every day. It was on their way to school. During the day, they stopped to stare. At night, they rushed past the house.

Everyone thought the house was creepy. But Javier wanted to go inside. He always dared his friends to go with him. They always said no.

Javier dared his friends to check out the creepy old house. ▶

One October night, Javier and his friends were walking home. They had been to a football game. There were many other kids around. One girl was new in town. No one had seen her before. She said her name was Tabitha.

"That's a cool name," Javier said.

"It's an old name," Tabitha said. She stared at Javier. She had a mean look on her face. Javier was a little bit freaked out. Tabitha looked tough. Maybe she was as tough as he was!

Javier hurried ahead of the group. He wanted to be in the lead. He had a plan.

Moments later, the kids reached the old house. Moonlight shone on its broken windows. They looked like eyes. They seemed to be staring at the kids. The group walked faster.

Javier stopped right in front of the house. "Who wants to go in?" he asked.

"I dare you."

"Oh, come on, Javier," one kid said. "You're just **bluffing**."

"No, I'm not," Javier said. "Come with me. I dare you."

"I'll go," a voice said. Everyone turned around. It was Tabitha. She walked up to Javier. She stared him in the eyes. Then she pulled open the rusty iron gate in front of the house.

Tabitha turned around. "Come on," she said to Javier. "Let's go."

Javier looked at his friends. Some of them made clucking sounds. They thought he was chicken!

"I'll show them!" Javier thought. He walked up to the rusty gate. He joined Tabitha on the other side.

"Okay," he said. He looked back at his friends. "I'll see you guys soon." He wanted to sound cool. But his voice was a little shaky.

The rest of the kids moved down the street. They wanted to get away from the house. Javier watched them. Then he turned to face Tabitha. She was smiling strangely.

"What's wrong?" she asked. "Are you afraid of ghosts?"

"I'm not afraid of anything," Javier said. "Are you scared?"

"No!" said Tabitha. She started toward the house.

Javier followed her. He had never been this close to the house before. It looked even creepier up close.

Tabitha walked up the steps. Javier followed her. The steps groaned under his feet.

Tabitha turned the knob on the front door. The door swung open. A cold, musty breeze rushed out.

"You first," Tabitha said to Javier. She waited for him to go in.

Javier's feet didn't want to move. He forced them to enter the house. It was dark inside. It was like a tomb. The front door slammed shut. Javier whirled around. Tabitha was standing right behind him.

She walked ahead. She went into a big room. Javier followed. In the moonlight, he saw a fireplace. There was an old piano, too. Tabitha ran her hand across the keys. The sound made Javier's heart beat faster.

Tabitha walked over to a staircase. She started up the steps.

"Come on," she said to Javier. It sounded like an order.

Javier didn't know what to do. He could run for the door. But Tabitha would tell his friends. They would all make fun of him.

Tabitha was already halfway up the stairs. Javier hurried to catch up.

"Where are we going?" Javier asked.

"You'll see," said Tabitha. She kept climbing. Soon, she reached the second floor of the house.

Javier had a sick feeling in his stomach. He wanted to run away. Then Tabitha looked back at him. Her eyes dared him to follow her.

Javier's feet felt heavy. He dragged them down the hallway. Tabitha waited there. She stood before an open door. It led to another flight of stairs. Javier wondered where they were going.

"Almost there," she said. She shut the door behind them.

Javier was finally inside the old house. Yet, he did not really want to be there. ▶

Tabitha pushed Javier forward. She slammed the door shut behind them. Then Javier heard a clicking sound.

"Did she just lock that door?" he wondered. He felt even more afraid.

The staircase was pitch dark. Javier stumbled up it. He stepped into the attic.

"Sit down," Tabitha said. She came up behind Javier in the dark. She pushed him down onto a chair.

All Javier could see was a small window. The sky outside was cloudy. Then the moon appeared. Javier looked around. In the moonlight, he could see other chairs.

Javier screamed! Who—or what— was sitting in those chairs? He was sure he could see a ghostly figure in each chair.

Tabitha walked in front of him. She smiled a **mocking** smile. "Now are you afraid of ghosts?" she asked.

Javier's heart began to beat faster. Tabitha seemed to be fading away.

Javier leaped up from his chair. He made a **desperate** run for the stairs. All around him, the ghostly creatures sat, staring. Javier was sure they were grinning at him. Their grins were **eerie.**

Javier raced down the steps. But was the door below unlocked? He pushed it as hard as he could. He gasped with relief when it flew open.

Javier raced out of the haunted house. He never dared anyone to go inside again!

Was everything that happened to Javier real? Did he get scared and imagine things? What do you think?

Kate buys a good luck charm. She gets more than she wished for.

2 | The Cat's Meow

Kate walked down the **deserted** street. She searched the buildings to her left and right. She was looking for a shop. She had read about it on the Internet.

Kate searched for a long time. But she could not find the shop. Then she heard a creaking sound over her head. She looked up. A sign was moving back and forth on rusty chains. On it was a picture of a cat. Kate read the words: *The Cat's Meow.* She had finally found the shop!

After a long search, Kate finally found the shop. ▶

Kate peeked in the window. The shop was dark and gloomy. Yet she knew it would have what she wanted. She pushed open the door. She went inside.

Kate walked through the shop. She looked around. She saw shelves and tables. They were cluttered with weird, old stuff.

Kate turned a corner. She heard a sound near her feet on the floor. It sounded like an animal scurrying past.

How creepy! Kate was about to walk out. But a voice stopped her.

"Can I help you?" The voice sounded kind. Kate turned around. She saw an old woman. The woman was standing at the back of the shop.

"I read about your shop online," Kate said. "I'm…I'm looking for a good luck charm. I really need one."

"So, you believe in luck," the woman

said. She seemed to read Kate's mind.

Kate nodded. "I'm having trouble in school," she said. "And my parents are angry about it. You must have something to help me."

The woman smiled. "You'll know your good luck charm when you see it," she said. "Take a look around. I'll sell you anything you want for ten dollars."

The old woman disappeared into a back room. Kate looked around. She saw a stuffed bird. It was sitting beside a human skull. Next to that was a book about UFOs.

"What a weird shop," Kate thought.

Kate walked around the shop. She picked up an object. Then she looked at another. Nothing seemed right. Kate felt a prickle of fear. She was sure someone was watching her!

Nervously, Kate picked up a black velvet box. Inside was a ring. It was shaped like a cat's face. It had two glittering, green eyes. They were made of jewels.

Kate stared at the ring. Somehow, she knew she had to have it. She really did know her good luck charm when she saw it. This ring was it!

The woman came back into the room. She saw the ring box in Kate's hand. She gasped.

"You don't want that ring," the woman said. "Put it down."

An eerie hiss came from the back of the shop. The sound scared Kate. But she held onto the box.

"I do want the ring," she said. "It is my good luck charm."

"That ring has special powers!" the woman warned. "You cannot control it."

Again, Kate heard an angry hiss. This time, she dropped the box. It landed on the counter.

"You should go now," the woman said. "Come back when you are ready to pick something else."

The woman turned away. She marched into the back room.

The ring was kind of scary. Yet Kate had to have it.

Kate stared at the ring. She just knew it would bring her luck. She reached into her bag. She pulled out a ten-dollar bill. She dropped it on the counter. Then she grabbed the box. Quickly, she slipped it into her pocket.

Kate looked around the shop. She felt scared. She turned and hurried out. Her heart was beating hard.

That evening, Kate could not concentrate on her homework. Instead, she looked at the ring. She was wearing it on her finger. Kate asked the ring to bring her good luck.

The ring just stared at her. Its green eyes glittered.

Finally, Kate turned off the lights. She crawled into bed. She tossed and turned. At last, she fell asleep.

Kate woke with a start. Her room was dark. She heard a weird sound. Her heart pounded. Something was creeping around her bed.

Kate wanted to scream. But she was too scared. She felt the ring burning her finger. She looked at it. The eyes were shining. They did not look like good luck now. They looked scary.

Kate pulled the ring off her finger. She hid it under her pillow.

Seconds later, a dark shadow jumped onto her bed. It hissed at her. Kate saw two glittering green eyes. They were coming toward her. It was the cat she had heard in the shop! The cat clawed at Kate's bedsheets. She knew it was looking for the ring!

Kate shook with terror. She saw the cat's eyes come closer. Kate shut her eyes. Finally, she found her voice. She screamed.

Kate's parents rushed into the room. They turned on the lights. Kate was still screaming. She begged her parents to look for the cat. But it had **vanished**! Her parents **assured** her she was only dreaming.

The next morning, Kate woke up in a **panic**. She looked under her pillow. The ring was still there.

Kate dressed in a hurry. She put the ring back into the black velvet box. She sneaked out of the house.

An hour later, Kate stood outside the old shop. She looked up at the cat on the creaking sign. Then she pushed open the door and walked inside. The old woman was standing behind the counter. She seemed to be waiting for Kate.

Kate pulled the velvet box out of her pocket. She put it on the counter.

"Please take it back," she said.

The woman gave Kate an eerie smile. "Do you still want a good luck charm?" she asked.

Kate shook her head. Then she turned and ran out of the shop. On the sidewalk outside, she looked back.

She saw the real cat. It was sitting by the window. Its green eyes were watching her.

Did the cat really come into Kate's room? Or was she dreaming?

Is Luke's new video game really just a game?

3 | Chomp!

Luke hunched in front of his computer. He had just downloaded a new game. It was called *The Maze of Mystery*.

Luke started the game. A dark image came onto the screen. Luke watched as it became clearer. It was the figure of a boy. He was standing in a hallway. Luke could see only his back. He began to **navigate** the figure down the hallway.

Whoosh. A huge, red monster appeared. It stood at the end of the

Luke battled a monster in the video game. ▶

hallway. Its jaws opened. It had sharp, pointed teeth.

Click. Luke **vaporized** the monster. But it had gotten close. Luke wiped beads of sweat from his forehead.

"Luke, what are you doing?" his mother asked. She was standing right behind him. Luke lost his concentration.

Chomp. Another creature ate him.

"It's a new game, Mom," Luke said. "And you just made me toast."

"You spend too much time on that computer," his mother said. "It's more real to you than real life!"

Luke wanted to start the game again. But he didn't want to prove his mom right. So he pulled his eyes away from the screen. He looked at his mom.

"We're going to the Walkers' house tonight," she was saying. "You could come along. Their son likes you."

Luke groaned. "Mom, that little kid is boring. I'd rather stay here by myself."

Luke's mother **hesitated**. "I don't like you being home alone."

"Don't worry about me, Mom," Luke said. "I'll stay right here in my room."

"Just don't play that game all night," his mom warned. Luke agreed. Then she walked away.

Click. Luke started the game again. The boy appeared. His back was to Luke. Would Luke ever see the boy's face?

Luke navigated the boy down the hallway. *Whoosh*. A different monster appeared. But it was just as terrifying. *Click*. The creature screamed. Then it disappeared.

Then the hallway opened to a staircase. A picture on the wall caught Luke's eye. "That's weird," he thought. "That picture looks just like the one by our stairs."

Chomp. For a second, he saw a scary face. It was the creature that ate him. Then the screen went black.

Click. Luke started the game again. He navigated the boy down the hallway. He tried hard to concentrate. Then he heard a bell ring.

At first, Luke thought the sound came from the game. Then he heard it again. He realized it was the doorbell.

Luke looked up from the screen. *Chomp.* A creature ate him.

Luke left his room. He walked down the stairs to the front door. On the way, he glanced at the picture hanging by the stairs. It was just like the one in the game. Freaky!

Luke hurried down the long hallway. He went to the front door. He looked through the peephole. His friend Alex was outside.

"My dad is taking me to a movie. Want to come with us?"

Luke almost said yes. But he wanted to get back to the game.

"I can't. I promised my parents I'd stay home tonight," Luke said.

"For real?" Alex asked. "Or do you just want to play video games all night?"

"No, really," said Luke. "I have to stay home." That was a lie. But Luke didn't care. He needed to get back to that game! He hurried back to his computer.

Click. The boy stood in the hallway. *Whoosh.* A creature rushed at him. *Click.* The creature disappeared.

Luke moved the boy toward the stairs. The picture was still there. Luke tried desperately to focus. *Whoosh.* Another monster rushed in.

Luke felt something touch him. He shuddered. *Click.* The creature on the screen screamed. Then it disappeared.

Luke moved the boy to the top of the staircase. Now Luke's fingers were shaking. He could still feel the cold, clammy hand that had touched him.

Whoosh. A creature appeared and grinned at him.

Click. The creature didn't disappear. It laughed at Luke and ran away.

Luke moved the boy down the hallway. *Whoosh.* It was the same monster. It escaped before Luke could click it.

Luke wanted to stop the game. His body was weak with fear. But he kept playing. His hand moved the boy down the hallway. The boy came to a door.

Luke stared at the screen. The boy opened the door. For the first time, Luke could see the boy's face. It was his own face! It was screaming.

Luke spun around. He saw the monster. It was coming straight for him—fast. *Whoosh*. *Chomp*!

> **Which story in this book was the scariest? Why?**

Luke spun around. He saw the monster coming toward him!

Glossary

assured *(verb)*: told someone something positive so that they worried less

bluffing *(verb)*: pretending to be in a stronger position than you really are

deserted *(adjective)*: empty and quiet because no people are there

desperate *(adjective)*: willing to do anything to change a bad situation

eerie *(adjective)*: strange and frightening

hesitated *(verb)*: paused

mocking *(adjective)*: making fun of

navigate *(verb)*: move or direct

panic *(noun)*: a sudden feeling of terror

vanished *(verb)*: disappeared

vaporized *(verb)*: changed into a vapor